The Tale
Proudfoot

Arthur Scott Bailey

THE TALE OF TURKEY PROUDFOOT

I

A STRUTTER

ALL the hen turkeys thought Turkey Proudfoot a wonderful creature. They said he had the most beautiful tail on the farm. When he spread it and strutted about Farmer Green's place the hen turkeys were sure to nudge one another and say, "Ahem! Isn't he elegant?"

But the rest of the farmyard folk made quite different remarks about him. They declared Turkey Proudfoot to be a silly, vain gobbler, noisy and quarrelsome.

Now, there was truth in what everybody thought and said about this lordly person, Turkey Proudfoot. He did have a huge tail, when he chose to spread it; and his feathers shone with a greenish, coppery, bronzy glitter that might easily have turned the head of anybody that boasted such beautiful colors. Certainly the hen turkeys turned their heads—and craned their necks—whenever Turkey Proudfoot came near them. And when he spoke to them, saying "Gobble, gobble, gobble!" in a loud tone, they were always pleased.

The hen turkeys seemed to find that remark, "Gobble, gobble, gobble!" highly interesting. But everybody else complained about the noise that Turkey Proudfoot made, and said that if he must gobble they wished he would go off by himself, where people didn't have to listen to him.

And nobody but the hen turkeys liked the way Turkey Proudfoot walked. At every step he took he raised a foot high in the air, acting for all the world as if the ground wasn't good enough for him to walk upon. And when he wasn't picking up a seed, or a bit of grain, or an insect off the ground, he held his head very high. Often Turkey Proudfoot seemed to look right past his farmyard neighbors, as if he were gazing at something in the next field and didn't see them. But they soon learned that that was only an odd way of his. Really, he saw about everything that went on. If anybody happened to grin at him Turkey Proudfoot was sure to take notice at once and try to pick a quarrel.

After all, perhaps it wasn't strange that Turkey Proudfoot should act as he did. Being the ruler of Farmer Green's whole flock of turkeys, he was somewhat spoiled. All the hen turkeys did about as he told them to do. Or if they didn't, Turkey Proudfoot thought that they obeyed his orders. And the younger gobblers as well had to mind him. If they didn't, Turkey Proudfoot fought them until they were ready to gobble for mercy.

Having whipped the younger gobblers a good many times, Turkey Proudfoot firmly believed that he could whip anything or anybody. And there was nobody on the farm, almost, at whom he hadn't dashed at least once. He had even attacked Farmer Green. But Farmer Green quickly taught him better. A blow on the head from a stout stick bowled Turkey Proudfoot over and he never tried to fight Farmer Green again.

That proved that Turkey Proudfoot wasn't as empty-headed as some of his neighbors thought him. It was possible to get a lesson into his head, even if one had to knock it into his skull with a club.

II

THE SILLY SIX

FARMER GREEN owned six geese. Though there was an even number of them, they were odd creatures. They had little to do with the other farmyard folk, but kept much to themselves. If one of them started up the road on some errand, the other five always followed her. If one of them suddenly took it into her head to enjoy a swim her five companions were sure to want one too, and waddled with her to the duck pond.

Now, Turkey Proudfoot never went swimming. Like all the rest of the flock over which he ruled, he thought swimming was bad for one's health. He couldn't understand how anybody could enjoy cold water, except for drinking purposes. And somehow he always felt as if his feathers had been a bit ruffled whenever he saw the six geese set out for the duck pond. Although their taking a swim was no affair of his, still it made him angry.

"Look at those geese!" he would gobble angrily to anybody that happened to be near him. "They're going to take another cold, wet bath. They're old enough to know better. I often wonder why Farmer Green wants such a stupid crew on his farm. The Silly Six, I call 'em!"

When Turkey Proudfoot talked in that fashion there were some that didn't agree with him. The ducks never failed to quack their displeasure. And old Spot sometimes growled and told him he'd be the better for a good swim.

But Turkey Proudfoot always declared, in answer to that, that he knew he'd catch his death of cold if he ever stepped into the duck pond. And there were some of the same mind as he.

There was Miss Kitty Cat, who never liked to get her feet wet and on stormy days lay by the hour beneath the kitchen stove and dozed.

And there was the rooster. He didn't believe in wet, cold baths. He liked dry dust baths. And when, one day, Turkey Proudfoot turned to him suddenly and gobbled, "There go the Silly Six to swim!" the rooster

4

answered with a sniff, "Well, let 'em go! Don't stop 'em on my account. I certainly don't want to join them."

Turkey Proudfoot was all ready for a quarrel. "I hope you don't think I want to go swimming with the geese," he retorted. There was a dangerous glitter in his eyes.

Seeing this, the rooster made haste to assure Turkey Proudfoot that he meant nothing of the sort.

"Don't let's quarrel!" the rooster cried—for he was much smaller than Turkey Proudfoot. "There's nothing for us to quarrel about. We're of the same mind about the geese and their swimming."

"I'm disappointed," Turkey Proudfoot told him. "For a moment I thought I had an excuse for fighting you. And I'm not sure that I oughtn't to be angry with you for agreeing with me when I didn't expect you to."

The rooster gave a hoarse crow. He thought Turkey Proudfoot was joking. And being afraid of Turkey Proudfoot, the rooster felt obliged to laugh loudly at his jokes.

"Don't laugh at me!" Turkey Proudfoot cried.

"C-c-can't I laugh at the six silly geese?" the rooster stammered.

"Yes!" said Turkey Proudfoot. "Yes—if you see anything funny about them. For my part, I couldn't laugh at them if I tried to. The mere thought of plunging into cold water almost gives me a chill."

III

THE MEDDLER

"WHY don't you tell the geese that it's dangerous for them to swim in the duck pond?" the rooster asked Turkey Proudfoot. "Tell them how it almost gives you a chill just to see them set out for the pond. Ask them to keep out of the water."

Turkey Proudfoot drew himself up to his full height, spread his tail, and looked down at the rooster with great disdain. "Ask!" he exclaimed. "I never ask anything of anybody. I'll have you know, sir, that I give orders. And when I give 'em I expect folks to obey 'em."

"Good!" cried the rooster gayly. He was really shaking in his shoes and didn't intend to let Turkey Proudfoot know it. "Order the geese to stay away from the water. Command them to stop swimming. If you don't, you'll have a terrible chill some day when you see them set out for the duck pond. And you don't want to be ill just before the holidays."

"That's true," said Turkey Proudfoot. "I don't want to get a chill and be ill." And then he turned suddenly upon the startled rooster. "Look here!" cried Turkey Proudfoot. "It seems to me thatyou are giving me orders."

"Not at all!" the rooster assured him. "No, indeed! You're mistaken."

"Don't tell me I'm mistaken!" Turkey Proudfoot bawled in an angry, gobbly voice. "I'm never mistaken."

"Oh, certainly not!" said the rooster, who was bold as brass with most of his neighbors, but very mild with Turkey Proudfoot.

"Ha!" Turkey Proudfoot exclaimed. "You're getting yourself into a hole, sir! If I wasn't mistaken, then you were giving me orders. And in either case I should have to fight you."

This was too much for the rooster. He couldn't grasp what Turkey Proudfoot was saying. He only knew that things looked bad for him because Turkey Proudfoot was getting angrier every moment.

6

"I say!" the rooster cried. "Please don't waste your time on me just now, Mr. Turkey Proudfoot! Here come the six silly geese back from the duck pond. And I'd suggest that you speak to them at once and warn them not to enter the water again."

Turkey Proudfoot glanced across the farmyard. It was as the rooster had said. The six geese were waddling around a corner of the barn in single file. Somehow the sight of them made him so furious that he forgot he had been picking a quarrel with the rooster.

"I'll attend to them," he gobbled. "I'll fix them. They'll be so scared that they won't dare leave this yard again."

Turkey Proudfoot hurried towards the geese. He didn't take time to strut, but ran across the yard with long strides.

"Don't be silly geese!" Turkey Proudfoot called. "Keep away from the duck-pond! The weather's getting colder every day; and it makes me shiver to see you start off for a swim."

Turkey Proudfoot had supposed the six geese would be very meek and most eager to obey his commands. But to his great surprise they stopped, wheeled about so that they stood in a row, facing him, and hissed loudly.

It was not at all the sort of answer Turkey Proudfoot had expected.

IV

SCARING THE GEESE

THE six geese stood in a row and hissed at Turkey Proudfoot. He was so astonished that any one of them could have knocked him over with a feather, almost. When he gobbled an order at them, telling them not to go swimming again, the geese hissed at him. That was just the same as telling him to keep still and mind his own affairs.

And Turkey Proudfoot was not used to answers like that.

The rooster had followed him across the farmyard in order to look on and listen while Turkey Proudfoot spoke to the geese. And his surprise was as great as Turkey Proudfoot's.

"Surely!" he muttered to Turkey Proudfoot, "you aren't going to let these geese go unpunished. They've insulted you."

"Ha! I thought they had," Turkey Proudfoot exclaimed. "And I'm glad to know that you agree with me. There's no doubt that they deserve a severe beating."

"Ah!" the rooster cried. "Now we'll see some fun."

"Yes!" said Turkey Proudfoot. "I expect we'll have a merry time." Still he made no move to attack the geese, who stood motionless, facing him like soldiers.

"Well!" the rooster said impatiently. "Aren't you going to punish these geese?"

"Certainly not!" Turkey Proudfoot cried. "Why did you tag after me across the yard if it wasn't to fight them? I've often heard that you were usually spoiling for a fight. So here's your chance!"

It was true, in a way, that the rooster was always ready to fight. Not one of the cockerels on the farm dared to speak to him. But he always took care to fight only such as he knew he could whip. Certainly he had no desire to fight six geese all by himself. He drew back a little and shook his head.

"This is not my quarrel," he declared.

"But you suggested it," Turkey Proudfoot reminded him. "And now I suggest that you take it up. I did my part. You must do yours."

A wild look came into the rooster's eyes. He wanted to run away. But he was a proud bird. He thought a great deal of the looks of things. And he didn't know just what to do.

Then something happened that suddenly made him act—and act quickly. The six geese all took one step forward.

The rooster turned tail and dashed around the barn, out of sight. And Turkey Proudfoot found himself facing the six geese, who soon took one more step towards him and hissed louder than ever.

He had never felt so ill at ease in all his life. But he remembered that he was the ruler of the turkey flock and the handsomest bird on the farm. It would never do to have it said that he ran away from six silly geese.

"I'll scare 'em," he thought. Thereupon he burst into a deafening gobble and took one step towards the geese.

He had fully expected to see them fall back. What they actually did was most annoying. Every one of them took another step towards him.

9

V

A SAFE PERCH

AS Turkey Proudfoot faced the six geese in the farmyard he began to feel that he had made a great mistake in speaking to them. Their hisses were far from agreeable. They were even threatening.

"This will never do," Turkey Proudfoot muttered to himself. "No doubt I could whip all six of them; but they'd be likely to pull some of my tail feathers out. And I don't want my tail spoiled." For a moment or two he didn't know what to do. But suddenly an idea popped into his head.

"Follow me!" he ordered the geese. And wheeling about, he marched off across the farmyard.

The geese waddled after him.

Perched on top of a wagon wheel in front of the barn, the rooster saw the odd procession. And he gave voice loudly to his delight.

"The geese are chasing Turkey Proudfoot!" he crowed. He called to everybody to hurry and see the fun. And all the hens came a-running.

"Nonsense!" said Turkey Proudfoot. "I ordered the geese to follow me. They're simply obeying orders." And he strutted, a little faster than usual, toward the tree near the farmhouse where he roosted every night.

"Halt!" he cried to the geese when they reached the tree. As he spoke, Turkey Proudfoot flapped himself up and settled on a low branch. At last he felt safe. He knew that the geese wouldn't follow him up there. With their webbed feet they never roosted in trees.

Meanwhile the hen turkeys had come a-running too, from the meadow. They wanted to see what was going on. And they promptly fell into a loud dispute with the rooster and the hens.

"He did!" the hens cackled, meaning that Turkey Proudfoot had run away from the geese.

10

"He didn't!" the hen turkeys squalled, meaning that Turkey Proudfoot hadn't been chased, but had led the geese across the farmyard.

The six geese took no part in the quarrel. They had driven Turkey Proudfoot into the tree. And knowing that he wouldn't come down so long as they waited there, they marched off in single file toward the duck pond.

"Where are you going?" the rooster asked them.

The leader of the geese turned her head at him and hissed. And her five companions turned their heads at him too, and hissed likewise.

"I ordered them to go and have a swim," Turkey Proudfoot cried from his tree, as soon as the geese were out of hearing. "I don't want them about the farmyard. I haven't time to bother with them. Besides, they're so stupid that I never could teach them anything. I walked ahead of them, across the farmyard, to show them the stylish strut. But they couldn't learn it. They'll waddle to the end of their days."

"There!" cried the hen turkeys to the hens. "You hear what he says. The geese weren't chasing him. He was trying to teach them to strut."

"Huh!" exclaimed Henrietta Hen, who always spoke her mind right out. "Turkey Proudfoot had better be careful. Some day those geese will teach him how to waddle."

VI

THE MIMIC

YOUNG Master Meadow Mouse had often peeped at Turkey Proudfoot from behind a clump of grass, or a hill of corn. But he had never dared show himself to Turkey Proudfoot. Somehow the old gobbler looked terribly fierce. And he was so big that Master Meadow Mouse didn't like the idea of even saying "Good day!" to him. He had heard Turkey Proudfoot spoken of as a "gobbler." Who knew but that a gobbler would gobble up young Master Meadow Mouse if he had a chance?

Unseen by everybody, Master Meadow Mouse had watched the geese drive Turkey Proudfoot across the farmyard and seen him flapping up to roost in a tree out of their reach. And though Turkey Proudfoot strutted and tried to act very lordly as he headed the procession across the yard, Master Meadow Mouse had noticed how Turkey Proudfoot kept a wary eye on the geese behind him, and stepped not quite so high as he usually did, but further.

"Ho!" Master Meadow Mouse had piped to himself in his thin voice. "Turkey Proudfoot is not the brave fellow I always thought him. He's afraid of geese!"

From that moment Master Meadow Mouse forgot his fear of Turkey Proudfoot. Nobody stands in awe of a coward. So the very next time that Master Meadow Mouse saw Turkey Proudfoot strutting in the yard he crept up behind Turkey Proudfoot and tried to walk exactly like him.

There were a good many farmyard fowls scratching about the yard at the time, and wishing to appear at his best, Turkey Proudfoot spread his tail, puffed out his chest, and strolled all around as if he — and and not Farmer Green — owned the place.

Although Turkey Proudfoot seemed to see none of his neighbors, nevertheless he was watching them carefully out of the corner of his eye, to see whether they were noticing him.

They were. There was no doubt of that.

Not only were they looking at him; they were laughing at him as well.

Turkey Proudfoot's face couldn't grow red with rage. It was red already. It was always red. Being very angry, he gobbled at the giggling hens, at the rooster, even at old dog Spot, "Why are you laughing at me?"

"We aren't!" they cried. "You've no reason to be angry with us."

"'Tis well," said Turkey Proudfoot with a toplofty toss of his bald head. "Since you're not laughing at me, you needn't laugh at all. I don't like your sniggering."

"We can't help laughing," a few of the more daring ones told him. "It's so funny!"

"What is?"

"He is!"

"Who is?"

"Master Meadow Mouse!"

"Master Meadow Mouse!" repeated Turkey Proudfoot in a bewildered fashion.

He looked in front of him. He looked to the left. He looked to the right. He couldn't see Master Meadow Mouse anywhere.

"Look behind you!" cried Henrietta Hen.

Turkey Proudfoot turned his head.

"I don't see any Master Meadow Mouse," he grumbled.

"How can you, when your tail's spread like that?" Henrietta Hen asked him. "Close up your tail and then you'll see what we're laughing at."

But Turkey Proudfoot declined to do anything of the sort.

"It's just a trick," he squalled. "You're all jealous of me and my beautiful tail. You don't want me to carry my tail this way."

Behind Turkey Proudfoot's tail Master Meadow Mouse did a very naughty thing. He stuck out his tongue. And all the onlookers shrieked with merriment.

VII

HALF WRONG

IT was no wonder that Turkey Proudfoot was angry. Everybody in the farmyard was laughing and looking his way — or so it seemed to him.

Since he couldn't see any joke, he decided to leave his silly neighbors and go off into the fields where he could be alone. So he walked slowly away, holding his head high and stepping in his most elegant manner.

To his great disgust peals of laughter followed him. And though he had intended to march off without saying a word, this last outburst so filled him with rage that he couldn't resist spinning about to glare and gobble at his tormentors.

He turned so quickly that he surprised Master Meadow Mouse with one of his tiny feet lifted high in the air. He surprised him so much that Master Meadow Mouse stood stock still and didn't even bring his foot down, but held it off the ground as if it had frozen stiff and couldn't be moved.

At first there was a most joyful look on Master Meadow Mouse's face. But it faded instantly into one of doubt and dismay. To tell the truth, Master Meadow Mouse hadn't expected Turkey Proudfoot to turn around and catch him right in his mimicking act.

"Ah, ha!" cried Turkey Proudfoot. "So it's you that they're laughing at, eh?"

Master Meadow Mouse was so upset that he murmured faintly, "Yes, it's me."

"Well, I don't blame them," said Turkey Proudfoot. "You certainly look very queer. Why are you holding your foot off the ground like that?"

"I was in the midst of taking a step when you turned around and startled me," Master Meadow Mouse explained. "And I don't know whether to set my foot down ahead of me, or to put it behind me."

15

"Don't be alarmed!" Turkey Proudfoot said. "I never fight folks of your size. You're too little for me to pay much attention to. I must say, however, that you have a very odd way of walking."

By this time Master Meadow Mouse had recovered from his surprise and wasn't afraid in the least. Now he laughed heartily.

"I was walking the way you walk," he cried.

"Oh, no!" Turkey Proudfoot exclaimed. "No, indeed! You certainly weren't." He didn't ask Master Meadow Mouse's pardon for contradicting.

"I'd like to know why I wasn't," Master Meadow Mouse replied somewhat hotly. "I was strutting right behind you, all the way across the yard. That's why everybody was giggling."

"It's no wonder they were poking fun at you," Turkey Proudfoot told him. "You amused the neighbors because you thought you were strutting, while you really weren't."

Master Meadow Mouse put his foot down on the ground. He was puzzled.

"I don't know why I wasn't strutting," he retorted. "I was raising my feet just as high as I could lift them."

"Ah, yes?" said Turkey Proudfoot. "But you forgot one thing."

"What was that?"

"You didn't spread your tail," Turkey Proudfoot explained. "And that's half of strutting."

"I—I didn't know it," Master Meadow Mouse stammered. And then he darted away, to hide in the grass beyond the fence.

He felt much ashamed to have made such a mistake.

VIII

HARD TO PLEASE

IT was very hard to please Turkey Proudfoot. To be sure, he always pleased himself. But nothing anyone else did seemed to suit him. And there was one thing that always made him peevish. That was the gobbling of the younger turkey cocks.

To anybody that wasn't a turkey, their voices sounded just as sweet as Turkey Proudfoot's. But he claimed that there was something wrong with all gobbles except his own. Either they were too loud or too soft, too high or too low, too long or too short. And whenever a young cock gobbled in his hearing Turkey Proudfoot was sure to rush up to him and order him to keep still, for pity's sake!

They usually obeyed him. Not only was Turkey Proudfoot the biggest gobbler on the farm, but he had a fierce and lordly look about him. It was a bold young turkey cock that dared defy him. Once in a while one of them foolishly ventured to tell Turkey Proudfoot to mind his own affairs. And then there was sure to be a fight—a quick, short, noisy fray which ended always in the same fashion, with Turkey Proudfoot chasing the young cock out of the farmyard.

Luckily for the youngsters, they could run faster than he could, for they were not nearly as heavy.

Although Turkey Proudfoot didn't like to hear others gobble, nevertheless he enjoyed the excuse for a fight that their gobbling gave him. And when he had nothing more important to do he often stood still and listened in the hope of hearing some upstart gobbler testing his voice in a neighboring field. Newly grown cocks had to go a long way off to be safe from Turkey Proudfoot's attacks.

One day in the middle of the summer the lord of the turkey flock was feeding behind the barn when a loud gobble brought his head up with a jerk.

17

"Ha!" Turkey Proudfoot cried. "That's somebody in the yard, around the barn. He thinks I'm further away than this, or he'd never dare bawl like that."

Turkey Proudfoot dashed around the barn at a swift trot. He was surprised to see not a turkey cock in the farmyard. The rooster was there, however. And Turkey Proudfoot eyed him sternly.

"You weren't trying to gobble a moment ago, were you?" he inquired.

"No, indeed!" said the rooster.

Turkey Proudfoot looked puzzled.

"Somebody gobbled," he declared. "I'm sure the noise came from this yard. I was behind the barn when I heard it. And I hurried around the corner at once."

"Maybe the person that gobbled ran around the other end of the barn, to dodge you," the rooster suggested.

"I'll go and see," said Turkey Proudfoot. And he went back where he came from.

He found nobody there. But that annoying gobble sounded again and brought him back into the yard even faster than before. "Who did that?" he squalled.

And somebody mocked him. Somebody repeated his question after him. It was the same voice that had gobbled.

Turkey Proudfoot's rage was terrible to see.

IX

A STRANGE GOBBLE

"GOBBLE, gobble, gobble, gobble!"

Turkey Proudfoot stood in the farmyard and craned his neck in every direction. That sound certainly was close at hand. Yet there wasn't a turkey cock anywhere in sight, either on the ground or in the trees.

Just for a moment Turkey Proudfoot was worried.

"That wasn't my gobble, was it?" he asked the rooster. "If I gobbled, I didn't know it."

"No! You didn't gobble," said the rooster, "though I must say that gobbling sounded a good deal like yours."

"Gobble, gobble, gobble, gobble!"

"There it goes again!" cried Turkey Proudfoot. He was almost frantic. "How can I fight that fellow if I can't see him?" he cried. He looked up at the roof of the barn; but there was no one there except the gilded rooster that told which way the wind blew. He looked up at the roof of the farmhouse.

"You don't suppose that fellow's hiding in the chimney, do you?" he asked.

"No doubt he is," said the rooster. "If I were you I'd fly up there and catch him."

"The roof's high for one of my weight to fly to," Turkey Proudfoot remarked.

"Still, I could flap up to the top of the woodshed and get to the roof of the house from there.... I'll take a look and see how high the house seems when I'm near it."

To the rooster's delight, Turkey Proudfoot started towards the house. The rooster promptly called to all the hens to "come quick," because Turkey Proudfoot was going to fly to the roof of the farmhouse. "I hope he won't get into trouble," said the rooster with a chuckle. "It would be a pity if he fell down the chimney."

In spite of his words, the rooster didn't look at all uneasy. Indeed, the only thing that worried him was the fear that Turkey Proudfoot wouldn't get himself into a scrape. But he thought it more polite not to say exactly what he hoped.

Turkey Proudfoot stalked up to the farmhouse and stopped near the piazza. He was gazing upwards and measuring the height of the roof with his eye when all at once a loud "Gobble, gobble, gobble, gobble!" almost tipped him over backward.

The outcry came from the farmhouse. There was no doubt of that. But it didn't come from the roof, nor the chimney.

Turkey Proudfoot stared at the windows and the doors and saw no one except Miss Kitty Cat, dozing on a window sill. Then something moved beneath the piazza ceiling. It was a cage, which swayed as a green figure clung to the wires on one side of it.

"I'm a handsome bird," a voice informed Turkey Proudfoot. "Gobble, gobble, gobble, gobble!"

For once in his life Turkey Proudfoot hadn't a word to say. For the moment he was struck dumb.

At last he found his voice. "Who are you?" he bellowed.

"Ha! ha! ha! ha!"

"Don't laugh at me!" cried Turkey Proudfoot.

"Polly wants a cracker," said the green bird.

A few quick steps brought Turkey Proudfoot upon the piazza, nearer the cage where the annoying green person swung and made queer, throaty noises — sounds which only angered Turkey Proud foot the more.

Turkey Proudfoot took a little run and rose into the air, to crash against the cage and then fall flapping upon the piazza floor.

The green person shrieked. And the hired man, with an axe in his hand, peered out of the woodshed door.

"Here, you old gobbler! You leave our Polly alone!" he called. And he ran out and gave Turkey Proudfoot a sharp rap with the axe helve.

Turkey Proudfoot ran off and hid behind the barn and sulked.

"There's a bird around here," he muttered, "that mocks Miss Kitty Cat; and they call him a Cat Bird. Now, here's a bird that mocks me; so I should think they'd call him a Turkey Bird. But they don't. I heard the hired man call him Pretty Polly.

"Pretty Polly indeed!" Turkey Proudfoot sniffed. "That creature is nothing but a bunch of green feathers and a loud voice."

X
THE WORM TURNS

HENRIETTA HEN had no love for Turkey Proudfoot. Beginning with the days of her chickenhood he had always ordered her about, telling her not to do this and not to do that. Even after she was grown up and had a family of her own, Turkey Proudfoot treated her as if she had just begun to scratch for herself.

If Henrietta Hen found a spot where somebody had spilled a few kernels of corn Turkey Proudfoot was more than likely to rush up to her and cry, "Go away! I've had my eye on that corn for some time. I saw it first."

On such occasions there was nothing Henrietta Hen could do except to stand aside and look on while Turkey Proudfoot ate the corn. He was so much bigger than she that he could bowl her over easily.

On her own account Henrietta didn't really think it worth while to try to make any trouble for Turkey Proudfoot. But when she led her first brood of chicks into the yard to teach them to find food for themselves, Turkey Proudfoot's lordly ways made her very angry.

"Move your family over on the gravel drive!" Turkey Proudfoot ordered her.

Henrietta Hen said flatly that she wouldn't.

"There are no bugs — no worms — in the gravel," she told him. "My chicks have a right to go anywhere on this farm."

Turkey Proudfoot looked at her in amazement. Never before had Henrietta Hen spoken to him in such a way.

"Hoity-toity!" he exclaimed. "Aren't you forgetting your manners, Henrietta?"

"No, I'm not!" she snapped. "I've stood too much from you all my life. I warn you now that the worm has turned."

Turkey Proudfoot glanced quickly down at the ground.

"Where's the worm?" he asked. "Point him out to me before he gets away."

"There!" cried Henrietta Hen. "That's just like you. If anybody spies a worm, you think you ought to have it."

"Come! come!" Turkey Proudfoot coaxed her. "Don't let's quarrel over a mere trifle such as a worm. Just you show me where you saw him turn and I'll show you how to snatch a worm up in the neatest and quickest fashion."

Henrietta Hen tossed her handsome head.

"The worm I was talking about is right before you," she sniffed. "If you can't see it, I shan't help you."

Of course she had been talking of herself when she remarked that the worm had turned. She had meant that she had always allowed Turkey Proudfoot to treat her like a worm under his feet. But at last she had made up her mind that he shouldn't order her about any longer.

Meanwhile Turkey Proudfoot was fast losing his temper.

"You've caused me to lose a fine, fat worm; and you shall suffer for it!" he scolded. "The only thing for you to do is to offer me a fine, fat chick in its place."

At that Henrietta Hen set up a great clamor.

"I'll do nothing of the sort!" she shrieked. And then she screamed for the rooster. "Come quick, Mr. Rooster! Help! Help!"

XI

BLUSTER

SOON after Henrietta Hen shrieked for the rooster he came hurrying around a corner of the barn. When he saw Turkey Proudfoot towering above Henrietta and her new brood of chicks in the middle of the farmyard he stopped short. To tell the truth, the rooster was afraid of Turkey Proudfoot and usually took pains to keep out of his way.

"Go back!" Turkey Proudfoot called to him. "You're not needed here. There's been a little difficulty; but I can settle it myself."

"Oh, very well!" the rooster replied. "I'm glad there's no great trouble. When I heard Henrietta calling me I thought she was in danger." He turned, then, to slink away behind the barn.

"Don't desert me!" Henrietta Hen besought him. "Help! Help!"

Turkey Proudfoot waved a wing at the rooster.

"Don't pay any attention to her!" he said. "She's excited. I'll have her calmed down in no time."

"Of course I'm excited!" Henrietta Hen cried. "Don't let him deceive you, Mr. Rooster! He's been threatening me!"

Turkey Proudfoot bade her, in an undertone, to be quiet.

"Go along about your business," he told the rooster. "She's mistaken. I haven't said I'd harm her."

"No! But he's talking about eating one of my chicks! And that's worse," Henrietta screamed. "If you're as brave as I always supposed, Mr. Rooster, you'll defend my family."

Although the rooster was terribly frightened, and wanted to run away, he simply couldn't desert Henrietta Hen.

"She's a nuisance," he muttered as he marched across the farmyard. "I don't see why she wanted to bring her chicks out here where Turkey Proudfoot would see them. She's landed me in a scrape. There won't be much left of me when that old gobbler gets through with me."

Nevertheless the rooster put on a bold front. Drawing himself up to look his tallest, he glared at Turkey Proudfoot and said shrilly, "What do you mean by annoying this lady?"

Turkey Proudfoot gulped. He wondered what had come over his neighbors. The rooster had always acted afraid of him. Though small, the rooster was strongly built. And he had a sharp bill and sharp spurs, too. Turkey Proudfoot noted these details carefully.

"I won't have to fight him," he thought. "I'll behave so fiercely that the rooster will be glad to run off. And then I'll run after him so folks will think I am chasing him."

Turkey Proudfoot then began to bluster. He gobbled loudly, without saying anything at all. He even made a few quick passes at the rooster with his bill.

To his dismay, the rooster merely dodged. He didn't turn tail and run, as Turkey Proudfoot had hoped he would.

"I'll have to try something else," Turkey Proudfoot said to himself. So he flapped his wings and jumped up and down and around the rooster.

The rooster was very ill at ease. But he didn't let Turkey Proudfoot know that. He kept turning about, so that he faced Turkey Proudfoot all the time. And he said to Henrietta Hen: "Gather your chicks and get them out of the way. There's going to be trouble here."

Henrietta Hen obeyed him without a word. And she had no sooner shooed her youngsters into the chicken house than Turkey Proudfoot gave a loud laugh—a somewhat forced, yet loud laugh.

"You're just the sort of bird I like," he told the rooster. "I've been testing you to see if you were brave. I'm delighted to find that you are. And I suggest that you and I stand by each other and run things in this yard to suit

25

ourselves. When folks don't do as I tell them to, you and I will attend to them."

"Agreed!" cried the rooster. He was greatly flattered. "We'll make the neighbors step lively." And off he went, to find Henrietta Hen and tell her how he and Turkey Proudfoot were going to help each other.

"You're even sillier than I supposed," she informed the rooster, to his great astonishment. He had expected nothing but praise from her.

He left her hurriedly. And he felt quite glum.

"She's just like the whole Hen family," he grumbled. "You never can tell what they're going to do or what they're going to say. They may squawk and cross the road; they may cross the road and not squawk; they may squawk and not cross the road; they may not cross the road and not squawk. I don't believe they know themselves what they are going to do next."

XII

MR. CROW'S NEWS

THERE was no denying that the rooster at Farmer Green's place had handsome tail feathers. But they were as nothing, compared with Turkey Proudfoot's. Not only were the rooster's fewer in number; but he couldn't spread them, fan-fashion.

Mr. Grouse, who lived in the woods, beyond the pasture, could spread his tail. But he was a much smaller bird than Turkey Proudfoot and his tail wasn't nearly as big.

Turkey Proudfoot often remarked that he had no rival. To be sure, there were young gobblers on the farm. But in the matter of tails, Turkey Proudfoot outshone them all.

Farmer Green once had another turkey cock that bade fair to have as fine a tail as Turkey Proudfoot's. And for a time this gentleman made Turkey Proudfoot feel a bit uneasy.

"I'll have to fight him and pull out some of his tail feathers," Turkey Proudfoot decided.

But on the very day, in the fall, when Turkey Proudfoot intended to pick a quarrel with this person — and spoil his fatal beauty — he was missing. And oddly enough, nobody ever saw him around the farmyard again.

Turkey Proudfoot went so far as to hint that he had scared the fellow away. Not many believed that that was what happened, however. For old dog Spot claimed to have seen one of the missinggobbler's wings hanging in the kitchen of the farmhouse.

"Mrs. Green uses it for a brush," Spot had explained.

When he heard that story Turkey Proudfoot exclaimed, "Nonsense! A Fox's tail is a brush. But a Turkey's wing is a wing. Old dog Spot doesn't know what he's talking about. No doubt Mrs. Green has a Fox's brush hanging up beside her kitchen range."

Still, most of the farmyard folks insisted that the missing gobbler had met with an accident. Anyhow, the question as to what had become of him didn't trouble Turkey Proudfoot. The fellow was gone. And there wasn't another young gobbler on the farm that was likely to have a tail out of the ordinary. So Turkey Proudfoot was content.

His peace of mind lasted only a few days. He was ranging through the meadow one morning when he heard a great commotion in the farmyard. Old Mr. Crow soon came sailing over from the edge of the woods to see what was the matter. And after a while he went sailing back again. On his way he stopped to drop down into the meadow and speak to Turkey Proudfoot.

"You ought to hurry home," Mr. Crow croaked. "Johnnie Green has a new pet. You ought to see him."

"Johnnie Green's pets don't interest me," Turkey Proudfoot sniffed. "He's never owned a pet yet that had a tail worth looking at twice. As for his Guinea Pigs—well, they haven't tails that you could look at even once. They haven't any tails at all. I must say I don't admire Johnnie Green's taste in pets," said Turkey Proudfoot.

"Ah! This one is different," Mr. Crow told him with a hoarse laugh. "When you see his tail you'll fold yours up in a hurry. And you'll never spread it again."

"Impossible!" cried Turkey Proudfoot. "Impossible!" He was so angry with Mr. Crow that he couldn't say anything more.

For all that, he strode away towards the farmyard. And he had a most uneasy feeling under his wishbone.

XIII

THE NEW PET

TURKEY PROUDFOOT came hurrying back to the farmyard from the meadow where Mr. Crow had stopped and advised him to go home and see Johnnie Green's new pet.

When Turkey Proudfoot scurried around the barn he found everybody all a-flutter. No one paid any attention to Turkey Proudfoot, though he spread his tail and strutted up to his neighbors with a most important air.

"What's going on here?" Turkey Proudfoot demanded in his most lordly tone.

Henrietta Hen went out of her way to answer him. "Johnnie Green has a new pet," she explained. "He's a wonderful creature."

"I don't think much of him," said the rooster. He had a surly look, as if something—perhaps a pebble—had stuck in his crop.

"I can't quite swallow this new pet," the rooster told Turkey Proudfoot.

"Ah! You haven't seen him with his tail spread!" Henrietta Hen exclaimed. "His tail is simply gorgeous."

His tail! That was exactly what old Mr. Crow had mentioned. "Oh, well!" Turkey Proudfoot thought. "I'm foolish to be stirred up over this affair. The new pet's tail can't be as grand as mine. There's nothing for me to worry about."

But there was. What Henrietta Hen said with her next breath made Turkey Proudfoot miserable.

"You'd better put down your tail," she advised him.

"Put down my tail!" he squawked. "Anybody would think you were talking about an umbrella. What's wrong with my tail, madam? I hope you don't think I'm ashamed of it."

"I fear you will be, when you see Johnnie Green's new pet," Henrietta Hen rattled on. "You'll want to hide your tail then."

"Stop!" cried Turkey Proudfoot sternly. "You have said too much."

"Good!" the rooster chimed in. "I agree with you. She always talks too much." Once such a remark about Henrietta Hen would have made the rooster angry. Now, however, it pleased him.

"I know what's the matter with you," Henrietta Hen told the rooster. "Your nose is out of joint."

"I beg your pardon," said the rooster. "My nose—and by that no doubt you mean my bill—isnot out of joint."

"Oh, yes it is!" she insisted. "And Turkey Proudfoot's will be out of joint too, as soon as he sees the newcomer."

"Where is he?" Turkey Proudfoot suddenly demanded. "Let me have a look at him! I'll soon show him whether there's anything wrong with my bill." He puffed himself up and looked very fierce.

To his amazement, Henrietta Hen only laughed.

"Tell that to the new pet!" she said. "You'll find him in front of the farmhouse."

Turkey Proudfoot didn't thank her. He was so angry that he was almost choking. And he strode off with a gleam in his eyes that the younger gobblers knew only too well—and feared.

On the lawn before Farmer Green's house Turkey Proudfoot saw such a sight as he had never expected to behold. A big bird stood proudly on the grass plot, looking for all the world as if he owned not only the house, but the whole farm. His colors were like the blues and greens of a rainbow. And behind him he carried aloft a tail that made Turkey Proudfoot all but ill with envy.

"Who-who-who is this person?" Turkey Proudfoot gasped, turning to old dog Spot.

"Don't you know?" said Spot. "He's Johnnie Green's new pet. He's the Peacock."

XIV

A PROUD PERSON

THE peacock in front of the farmhouse paid no heed to Turkey Proudfoot, but moved very slowly and very haughtily about the lawn. His huge tail was spread like a sail. In the light summer breeze it swayed and rippled, sending out a thousand shimmering gleams. And on his tail were dozens of eyes. At least they looked like eyes to Turkey Proudfoot. And they all seemed to be trying to out-stare him.

For a minute or two Turkey Proudfoot glared at this newcomer—this new pet of Johnnie Green's. Then, after first spreading his own tail to its fullest size, he swaggered up to the peacock.

"You needn't pretend not to see me," Turkey Proudfoot gobbled. "You can't fool me. You've a hundred eyes on your tail. And they've been looking at me steadily."

The peacock calmly turned his head and glanced at Turkey Proudfoot. He did not answer.

Turkey Proudfoot thrust his own head forward.

"Maybe I'm not good enough for you to speak to," he began. "Maybe I'm not enough of a dandy—"

Just then somebody interrupted him. It was Henrietta Hen. Being a prying sort of person she had followed Turkey Proudfoot around the house to see what happened when he and the newcomer met.

"Don't be rude to this gentleman," said Henrietta Hen. "He hasn't spoken since he arrived in the wagon an hour ago. We've about decided that he is dumb. And it's a great pity if he is. No doubt his voice—if he had one—would be as beautiful as his tail."

At that the peacock opened his mouth. Out of it there came the harshest sounds that had ever been heard on the farm. Turkey Proudfoot was so startled that he threw his head into the air and took several steps

31

backward. As for Henrietta Hen, she cackled in terror and ran out of the yard and crossed the road, where she narrowly escaped being run over by a passing wagon.

"My goodness!" Turkey Proudfoot thought. "It's no wonder this Peacock doesn't talk much. If I had a voice like his I'd never use it." He didn't know what the peacock had said. Somehow his voice was so awful that Turkey Proudfoot had caught no actual words that meant anything to him.

Again the peacock screamed. Henrietta Hen heard him. And she was so flustered that she ran back and forth across the road three times and was almost trampled on by a horse.

At last Turkey Proudfoot understood what the peacock said. "Are you a barnyard fowl?" he had asked.

"Yes, I am," said Turkey Proudfoot. "Aren't you?"

"No!" the peacock replied. "My place is out here in front of the house where people can see me when they drive by.... Probably," he added, "we shan't see much of each other."

So saying, he walked stiffly away and mounted the stone wall, where passing travellers would be sure to notice him and admire his beauty.

All this was a terrible blow to Turkey Proudfoot. For a moment he was tempted to rush at the haughty stranger and tear his handsome feathers into tatters. But the peacock looked so huge, standing on top of the wall with his great tail rising above him, and his voice was so frightfully loud and harsh, that Turkey Proudfoot didn't even dare threaten him. And that was something unusual for one who had long claimed to be ruler of the farmyard.

XV

MRS. WREN'S ADVICE

TURKEY PROUDFOOT never knew that the peacock was no bigger than he was. The elegant creature had such a huge tail and such a loud, harsh voice that Turkey Proudfoot stood in great awe of him.

Being very peevish, after his first meeting with the peacock, Turkey Proudfoot went behind the barn and found a young gobbler and gave him a terrible drubbing. Then Turkey Proudfoot felt better.

That night he roosted in a tree near the farmhouse. And in the morning when he awoke no thought of the peacock entered his head. He indulged in a few early morning gobbles — according to his custom — when a rasping scream reminded him of his hated rival. The peacock had slept in another tree not far away, even nearer the farmhouse than Turkey Proudfoot's.

"Huh!" said Turkey Proudfoot. "Farmer Green won't care for that racket every morning just outside his window. And neither will Rusty Wren. He always goes to the trouble of waking Farmer Green with his singing. This new pet of Johnnie's has taken it upon himself to do Rusty's work."

It was true that Rusty Wren was upset. He scolded a good deal to his wife that day about the peacock.

"There's no use of my singing a dawn song beneath Farmer Green's window any more," Rusty Wren grumbled. "The terrible squalls of this new bird will disturb everybody in the valley."

"Don't be silly!" said Mrs. Wren. "Don't be silly like Turkey Proudfoot. He's making himself miserable because the Peacock has a tail that sticks up higher than his. How absurd," she cried, "to be proud like Turkey Proudfoot, just because your tail happens to stick up in the air. Why, yours and mine stick up. But we don't go around boasting about them. And if somebody else has a stickier-up tail, why worry about it? And if somebody else with a louder voice can wake Farmer Green better than you can, why worry about that? Let the Peacock scream if he wants to!"

"And I—" cried Turkey Proudfoot, who had been standing beneath the tree where Mr. and Mrs. Wren were talking—"I say, let the Peacock parade in the front yard if he wants to. I certainlyshan't visit him there. I'll parade behind the farmhouse."

When Turkey Proudfoot first spoke up like that, Rusty Wren and his wife gave each other an uneasy look. They had expected him to be angry. And now, with an air of great relief, Mrs. Wren exclaimed:

"I apologize to you, Mr. Turkey Proudfoot. You're not as silly as I supposed. You're not as vain as I thought you were. I begin to think we've been mistaken about you all these years."

"You certainly have been," Turkey Proudfoot declared. "I'm not vain at all and I'm glad I haven't the Peacock's horrid, harsh voice. Mine is much more beautiful than his. And nobody can deny it."

"Gobble, gobble, gobble, gobble!"

XVI

DRUMMING ON A LOG

TURKEY PROUDFOOT was not always content to stay in the farmyard. Although Farmer Green fed him well, he liked to range over the fields in search of extra tidbits, such as grain, seeds and insects. Sometimes he wandered even as far as the pasture. And one day he strayed into the edge of the woods beyond the pasture fence.

There he discovered a beech tree. And Turkey Proudfoot was enjoying the nuts that he found on the ground beneath it when all at once a thump-thump-thump startled him. He raised his head and listened. The thumping sound came faster and faster, then died away in a rumble.

"Ho! It's only Johnnie Green drumming. Probably his mother wouldn't let him drum near the farmhouse, so he came to the woods where she couldn't hear him."

Turkey Proudfoot paid no more heed to the drumming, which rolled through the woods now and then. He went on with his search for beechnuts. But at last a thought popped into his head. "Johnnie Green must be eating most of the time, or he'd drum oftener," Turkey Proudfoot muttered. "He must have found a beech tree."

Soon Turkey Proudfoot decided to join Johnnie Green. He hoped that beechnuts were more plentiful beneath Johnnie's tree. So Turkey Proudfoot picked his way slowly through the underbrush. And guided by the thump-thump-thump which once in a while boomed upon his ears, at last Turkey Proudfoot came into a little clearing.

There on a log sat a speckly, feathered, short-necked gentleman with a tail spread in much the fashion in which Turkey Proudfoot so often carried his own.

Turkey Proudfoot drew back behind a bush, out of sight.

"I'll show that bird a tail that is a tail," he muttered to himself. So he spread his tail and then stepped proudly forth. A dry twig snapped beneath his weight. At that sound the stranger on the log turned his head quickly. Just for an instant there was an eager look on his face. But when he beheld Turkey Proudfoot it changed to one of disappointment.

"Who are you?" the stranger asked in none too pleasant a tone.

"I'm Turkey Proudfoot," said the ruler of the farmyard. "I live down the hill at Farmer Green's place."

"Then you'd better go home where you belong," said the stranger on the log. "I was expecting some one. I've been drumming for a friend. And when I heard you step on that dry twig I thought she'd come. I had my tail spread in her honor."

"Drum again!" Turkey Proudfoot ordered. "Call your friend at once and I'll show her a tail that is a tail. Yours is no bigger than Mrs. Green's fan."

The stranger made no move to obey. He appeared somewhat sulky.

"What's your name?" Turkey Proudfoot demanded.

"I'm Mr. Grouse," the stranger snapped out. "I supposed everybody in Pleasant Valley knew me. My drumming is famous."

"Indeed!" said Turkey Proudfoot. "I thought it was Johnnie Green making that noise."

"No wonder!" Mr. Grouse sniffed. "You're only a barnyard fowl. You can't be expected to know anything about us game birds."

XVII

A GAME BIRD

MR. GROUSE moved back and forth upon his log in the clearing in the woods. And casting a withering glance at Turkey Proudfoot, he said, "It's plain that you don't know what a game bird is. Men — and boys, too — come into the woods with guns to hunt us. And we make game of them by rising swiftly with a loud whir and flying off before they have time to shoot us."

Turkey Proudfoot gaped at Mr. Grouse.

"Don't they ever hit you?" he faltered.

"They've never shot me," said Mr. Grouse. "Once a hunter knocked out one of my tail feathers. But that was only an accident."

"I shouldn't care to be a game bird," Turkey Proudfoot remarked. "I'm sure it's much safer living at the farmyard."

Mr. Grouse gave him an odd look. One winter when food was scarce in the woods he had flown down to the farmyard. And he remembered seeing turkey feathers scattered about the chopping block near the woodpile.

"How do you usually spend the holidays?" he asked.

"Last Fourth of July I went up in the haymow and kept out of sight all day," said Turkey Proudfoot. "I don't like firecrackers."

Mr. Grouse nodded his head.

"I don't blame you for that," he observed. "Firecrackers sound too much like guns.... But I wasn't thinking of the Fourth of July," he went on. "When I asked how you spent the holidays I was thinking more of those to come. Now, Thanksgiving Day isn't a long way off. Have you made any plans for that?"

When he mentioned Thanksgiving Day Turkey Proudfoot gave a sudden start.

"For goodness' sake, don't speak of that now!" he cried. "I came to the woods to enjoy myself. And now you're trying to spoil my good time."

Mr. Grouse could see that Turkey Proudfoot was angry. And being rather peppery himself, he was tempted to say something sharp—something about axes, which are always sharp unless they're dull. But Mr. Grouse managed to control his temper. After all, he thought, it was no wonder that Turkey Proudfoot didn't want to hear about Thanksgiving Day.

"Pardon me!" said Mr. Grouse. "I only brought up this matter in a cousinly kind of way."

"Cousinly!" cried Turkey Proudfoot. "You and I, sir, are total strangers to each other."

"Well, we ought not to be," said Mr. Grouse. "It's time we got acquainted with each other. Didn't you know that your family and mine are related?"

"No!" Turkey Proudfoot exclaimed. "No! I never knew it."

"It's the truth," Mr. Grouse told him. "Don't you think we look a bit alike, except that my neck is somewhat short, and yours is long and skinny? And of course my head is feathered out, while yours is bald and red."

"That will do!" Turkey Proudfoot gobbled angrily. "Even if you are my cousin you needn't make such remarks about me."

Mr. Grouse begged his pardon again.

"I was only pointing out the differences between us," he explained. "But if they displease you, I'll speak of the ways in which we are alike. Now, take our tails—"

"I won't!" Turkey Proudfoot squalled. "I'll take my own tail wherever I go. But I won't take yours."

XVIII

RED LIGHTNING

"WHAT'S the matter with my tail!" cried Mr. Grouse.

"It's too small," Turkey Proudfoot declared. "Now, if you want to see a tail that is a tail—"

"I don't!" cried Mr. Grouse. "Not if you want me to look at yours! In fact, I don't care to talk with you any more. I was going to suggest a pleasant way for you to spend Thanksgiving Day. But nothing I say seems to please you. Besides, you began to boast about your tail the moment you entered this clearing. And if there's anybody I can't endure, it's a boaster." He was a rough and ready sort of fellow—this Mr. Grouse. When he had anything to say he didn't go beating about the bush. He came right out in the open and spoke his mind freely.

You might think that Turkey Proudfoot would have taken his cousin's remarks to heart. But he didn't. He was so pleased with his own tail that to him it was the biggest thing in the world. Indeed, when he spread his tail and looked at it he could see nothing else.

"You are jealous," he told Mr. Grouse. "And I can't blame you. It's only natural that you should look at my tail with envy. Everybody does down at the farmyard."

Turkey Proudfoot must have forgotten all about the peacock, when he spoke. Anyhow, he gazed around at his tail with great admiration.

All at once there was a terrible, loud whirring sound. Turkey Proudfoot started up in alarm. To his amazement, where Mr. Grouse had been sitting on the log there was now nothing at all.

"Up! Up!" It was Mr. Grouse's voice that Turkey Proudfoot heard; and it seemed to come from the tree right above his head.

Although Turkey Proudfoot didn't like to obey anybody's orders—and certainly not Mr. Grouse's—there was a note of alarm in the cry that made

39

him squall with terror. He started to run, flapping his wings awkwardly. And just as he rose into the air a reddish, brownish streak flashed beneath him.

Turkey Proudfoot settled himself on a branch of an old oak and looked down at a sharp-faced, grinning person who leered up at him. It was Tommy Fox. And though he looked very pleasant, inside he was feeling quite peevish. If it hadn't been for Mr. Grouse's warning he would surely have captured Turkey Proudfoot.

It was like Turkey Proudfoot not to thank his cousin. And it was like him, too, to fly into a rage.

"You might have warned me sooner," he complained to Mr. Grouse. "That red rascal is quick as lightning. He almost caught me."

"I thought you'd follow me when you saw me rise," said Mr. Grouse.

"I didn't see you."

"Well, you heard me, didn't you?"

"I heard a whirring sound," said Turkey Proudfoot, "but I didn't know what it was."

"Great snakes!" cried Mr. Grouse. "Farmer Green ought not to let you come into the woods—not if he expects you to spend Thanksgiving Day with him!"

Tommy Fox chuckled at that remark.

But Turkey Proudfoot never let on that he heard it. He crouched lower upon the limb of the oak tree and pretended to fall asleep.

Daylight was fast fading.

XIX

NIGHT IN THE WOODS

MR. GROUSE and Tommy Fox soon went about their business, leaving Turkey Proudfoot to roost in the oak tree in the woods.

Though he pretended to be fast asleep, Turkey Proudfoot had kept one eye slightly open. He had seen Tommy Fox trot away toward the pasture. He had heard Mr. Grouse go whirring off into the depths of the woods.

"It's too late to go back to the farmyard this evening," Turkey Proudfoot grumbled. "It's almost dusk already. And there's no telling about Tommy Fox. He may be hiding behind a tree, ready to pounce on me the moment I alight on the ground."

Turkey Proudfoot actually began to feel a bit sleepy. He was in the habit of going early to roost anyhow. So he huddled low on the branch of the oak tree. And soon he was in the land of dreams.

He slept a long time. And while he slept a number of things happened of which he knew nothing.

Tommy Fox came stealing back in the moonlight and gazed up at him with longing eyes.

Miss Kitty Cat, who had prowled through the pasture on a hunt for field mice, spied him. "I declare, that's Turkey Proudfoot!" she exclaimed. "He must have got lost up here. I certainly shan't wake him and tell him the way home. If I spoke to him he'd be sure to gobble and scare away all the mice in the neighborhood."

Benjamin Bat came zigzagging through the air and all but blundered into Turkey Proudfoot. Missing him by the breadth of a wing, Benjamin Bat hung head downward from a near-by limb and stared at the sleeping form. "Hello!" he squeaked. "Here's a newcomer in these woods. I should think he'd cling to that limb upside down. He'd find it a much safer way than sitting on top of the limb." Benjamin Bat was on the point of rousing

Turkey Proudfoot and advising him to change his position when a quavering whistle sent Benjamin hurrying away. He knew the voice of Simon Screecher, Solomon Owl's small cousin. And he had no wish to meet him.

Turkey Proudfoot stirred in his sleep. He was dreaming—dreaming that Johnnie Green was whistling to old dog Spot to come and drive Turkey Proudfoot out of the newly planted cornfield. The whistling seemed to come nearer and nearer. "I won't stir for old Spot," Turkey Proudfoot gobbled aloud in his sleep.

"Maybe you'll stir for me," cried a strange voice. And Turkey Proudfoot woke up with a start.

"Where am I?" he bawled. For a moment he couldn't remember having gone to sleep in the woods.

"You're right up under Blue Mountain," said Simon Screecher. "It's a dangerous place for a stranger to sleep. There are birds and beasts a-plenty in these woods that would make a meal of you if they caught you here."

Turkey Proudfoot yawned.

"I'm not worrying," he replied. "Foxes can't climb trees. And I'm as big as any bird in the neighborhood."

"You're as big—yes! And bigger than most!" Simon Screecher admitted. "But it isn't bigness alone that counts in the woods," he insisted.

"What does count, then?" Turkey

Proudfoot demanded.

"You ought to be able to guess," said Simon Screecher. "It's right in front of your eyes."

XX

BEAKS AND BILLS

TURKEY PROUDFOOT was a poor guesser. There in the woods, at night, Simon Screecher the owl had told him of something that "counted," something that was right in front of Turkey Proudfoot's eyes. And Turkey Proudfoot named everything he could think of. He mentioned the oak tree in which he sat, the darkness, the yellow moon.

"You're wrong!" Simon Screecher kept telling him. "You're getting further away with every guess. I suppose I'll have to tell you what I mean: it's your beak. And if that isn't right in front ofyour eyes, I don't know what is."

"My beak!" cried Turkey Proudfoot. "I don't call my bill my beak. I call my beak my bill."

"Well, beak or bill, yours is a useless thing," Simon Screecher sneered. "It may do well enough to pick up a kernel of corn. But it can't be much good as a weapon. It ought to be sharp and hooked to be of any use in a fight."

With every word that Simon Screecher said, Turkey Proudfoot was growing angrier.

"There's nothing wrong with my bill," he clamored. "I've had plenty of fights in the farmyard. The fowls are all afraid of me at home."

Simon Screecher gave a most disagreeable laugh.

"I wasn't thinking of farmyard fights," he sniffed. "If Fatty Coon or Grumpy Weasel or my cousin Solomon Owl grabbed you, you'd find that a fight in the woods is a very different matter from a mere barnyard squabble."

Turkey Proudfoot was furious.

"If you'll come over here on this limb I'll peck you," he cried.

"Huh! We don't fight that way in the woods," Simon Screecher retorted. "We don't peck. We tear-r-r-r!"

He rolled out the last word in a long-drawn quaver which gave it a horrid sound—especially in the woods, after dark. And Turkey Proudfoot felt chills a-running up and down his back.

"A-ahem! You-you needn't bother to come over here," he stammered. "I-I shouldn't like to peck you. You-er-you seem to be a very pleasant sort of person."

"Well, I'm not!" Simon Screecher informed him. "And you ought to see my cousin, Solomon Owl. He's a terrible fellow."

Turkey Proudfoot's wishbone seemed to be trying to come up into his mouth. At least, he had to swallow several times before he could answer.

"I'd like to see your cousin," he replied, "but not to-night."

He had scarcely finished speaking when a loud call came booming through the woods: "Whooo-whoo-whoo, whoo-whoo, to-whoo-ah!"

"Who's that?" gasped Turkey Proudfoot.

"That's my cousin, Solomon Owl," Simon Screecher explained. "And he's not far away."

"My goodness!" Turkey Proudfoot exclaimed. "If he's as big as his voice he must be enormous."

"He's twice my size," said Simon Screecher. "Not nearly as big as you are, of course! But you ought to see his beak. I do believe he could tear you into—"

"I don't want to see him to-night," Turkey Proudfoot interrupted. "I hope he won't come this way. Go and find him. And tell him to meet me here to-morrow night."

XXI

FARMYARD MANNERS

"OH, very well!" said Simon Screecher to Turkey Proudfoot. "I'll give my cousin your message. I'll tell him that you want him to meet you here in this clearing in the woods to-morrow night." So off Simon Screecher flew.

He had not been gone long when a noisy "haw-haw-hoo-hoo" rolled and echoed through the woods.

"He's laughing!" Turkey Proudfoot exclaimed. "Solomon Owl is laughing. I wonder what the joke is." He was so curious to know that he actually began to wish that Simon Screecher would hurry back. And after a little while he did.

"What was the joke?" Turkey Proudfoot demanded. "I heard you cousin laughing."

"Solomon Owl says that he doesn't care to meet you at all," Simon Screecher explained. "He says he has heard about you before and that you're a tough old bird."

"I'm not!" Turkey shrieked. "I'm very tender — and I'm not ten years old."

"Solomon Owl says he doesn't care to bother with any but the very youngest Turkeys."

"Well," Turkey Proudfoot retorted, "no matter what he says, the joke's on him. I wasn't coming back here to-morrow night. I don't like sleeping in the woods and having my rest disturbed by hoots and whistles."

"I suppose you don't," Simon Screecher admitted. "And I shouldn't care to try to sleep at the farmyard in the daytime and he waked by gobbles."

"I wish you would come down to the farmyard," Turkey Proudfoot told him. "You'd drive old dog Spot half crazy with your whistling."

Simon Screecher looked thoughtful.

"No!" he said. "Farmer Green might drive me half crazy with his old shotgun." He yawned as he spoke. "I don't see what's making me so sleepy," he remarked. "I must be going home."

"Don't hurry!" Turkey Proudfoot begged him. "I'm beginning to enjoy your company—though I can't exactly say why. And I'd like to gabble with you for an hour or two. I don't see what makes me so wakeful."

Just then a familiar sound greeted Turkey Proudfoot's ears. It was a crow. It was the rooster's crow, way down at the farmyard.

"Why, it's almost dawn!" Turkey Proudfoot exclaimed. "I didn't know the night was so nearly gone. It's no wonder I couldn't sleep. The dawn of another day always makes one wide awake."

"It always makes one sleepy, you mean," Simon Screecher corrected him.

Now, Turkey Proudfoot always grew angry when anybody corrected him in any way. And he flew into a rage.

"Go away! Go home!" he spluttered. "I don't enjoy your company."

Simon Screecher started homewards at once.

"Farmyard manners!" he muttered. "I declare, I wish Cousin Solomon hadn't eaten those two mice and those three frogs and those four spiders and those five grasshoppers to-night. When he's well fed he's always good-natured. If he had been hungry he'd have been in a terrible temper. And he'd have fought this Turkey bird until there was nothing left of him but his tail feathers."

Turkey Proudfoot never knew what a narrow escape he had. As soon as it began to grow light he dropped down out of the oak tree and hurried home, for he didn't want to miss the breakfast that Farmer Green always gave him.

Along in the fall, breakfasts always seemed to be bigger.

XXII

CRANBERRY SAUCE

"HO, hum!" old Mr. Crow yawned. He had stopped to talk with Turkey Proudfoot in the cornfield. It was fall; and the shocks of corn stood on every hand like great fat scarecrows, with fat yellow pumpkins lying at their feet, as if the scarecrows' heads had fallen off.

Mr. Crow always yawned a good deal when he chatted with Turkey Proudfoot and he wasn't always as careful as he might have been about covering up his yawns. Somehow Mr. Crow found Turkey Proudfoot dull company. Turkey Proudfoot had never been off the farm. On the other hand, old Mr. Crow was a great traveller. In his younger days he used to spend every winter in the South. And though he felt that the long journey had become too hard for him now, he thought nothing of flying around Blue Mountain and up and down Pleasant Valley.

As a result of his wanderings Mr. Crow had learned many things. And as a result of his staying at home, Turkey Proudfoot had learned little or nothing. Often Turkey Proudfoot complained to Mr. Crow that he couldn't even understand what Mr. Crow was talking about. But on this occasion Mr. Crow mentioned something that made him shudder.

"Ho, hum!" Mr. Crow yawned again. "My appetite isn't what it used to be. I believe I need to eat something tart. So I think I'll go over to the cranberry bog and pick a few cranberries. Why don't you come along with me?"

"Ugh!" Turkey Proudfoot exclaimed. "Cranberries! I can't stand even the mention of them."

"Ha!" Mr. Crow murmured to himself. "I've waked him up at last. I thought that would fetch him." And to Turkey Proudfoot he said, "Do you mean to tell me that you don't like cranberries? Why, I've always heard Turkey and cranberry sauce mentioned together."

"Ah!" said Turkey Proudfoot. "I've no doubt you've heard them spoken of only too often. But that's no reason why I should be fond of cranberry sauce. To tell the truth, all my life I've schemed to keep away from it."

"Then you don't care for the sharp taste of cranberries," said Mr. Crow.

"I've never eaten any," Turkey Proudfoot told him. "I'm sure I couldn't eat any if I wanted to. I believe the sight of them would take my appetite away."

Old Mr. Crow shook his head. And he leaned over to pick up a stray kernel of corn.

"Don't take that!" Turkey Proudfoot warned him. "I've had my eye on that kernel. I was going to eat it as soon as you went away."

Old Mr. Crow bolted the kernel of corn in a twinkling.

"You forget that you're not in the farmyard," he said boldly. "You can't treat me as if I were a Hen." And he chuckled — in a croaking sort of fashion.

Turkey Proudfoot glared at him. He knew that it was useless to rush at Mr. Crow. The old gentleman would only rise into the air and sail away with a loud haw-haw.

Now, Mr. Crow was a famous tease. He dearly loved to annoy others. And he gave Turkey Proudfoot a sly glance.

"Ouch!" he exclaimed. "I have a twinge of rheumatism."

"Where is your pain?" asked Turkey Proudfoot.

"In one of my drumsticks," said old Mr. Crow promptly, with a spluttering cough, to keep from laughing.

Turkey Proudfoot was furious.

"Cranberry sauce and drumsticks!" he exclaimed. "You do choose the most painful things to talk about."

"I was only trying to be polite," Mr. Crow told him. "You're always complaining that I don't talk about matters you can understand."

"I understand these only too well — " Turkey Proudfoot said — "especially at this season of the year!"

XXIII

VACATION TIME

IT was well along in November. And Turkey Proudfoot was feeling fidgetty. Whenever Farmer Green or the hired man stepped into the yard, he started up with a wild look in his eye.

Turkey Proudfoot was no longer roosting at night in the tree near the farmhouse.

With the coming of cold weather he had been glad enough to roost under a shed beside the barn.

Ever since the winter before, Turkey Proudfoot had enjoyed sound sleeps at night. But for weeks now he had often waked up in the middle of the night and found himself all a-shiver.

"It's the fault of that horrid old Mr. Crow," Turkey Proudfoot complained to old dog Spot one day. "He would talk about cranberry sauce and drumsticks. And of course a person can't sleep well with such things on his mind."

Old dog Spot nodded.

"Isn't it about time for you to go on your yearly vacation?" he inquired.

"Don't talk so loud!" Turkey Proudfoot hissed. And he took a quick glance all around. Then he said to old dog Spot, in almost a whisper, "To-morrow morning I'll be missing. Now, don't tell anybody!"

"Certainly not!" Spot promised. "I'm glad you're going away for a little change. I've thought lately that you were getting more peevish and quarrelsome than ever."

"I'm not!" Turkey Proudfoot gobbled. "I may be a bit excitable because I've lost a good deal of sleep lately. But I'm as good-natured as I ever was."

"Oh, very well!" said Spot. "I'll admit all that. I certainly don't want to quarrel with you just as you're going to leave us for a while.... We shall miss you while you're gone," he added with a sly smile. "The place will seem very quiet without your gobble."

"Yes, I dare say it will be lonesome around here," Turkey Proudfoot agreed. "And I suppose things will be in a muddle in the farmyard by the time I get back, with nobody to keep order there."

"I'll do the best I can while you're away," old dog Spot promised.

Turkey Proudfoot seemed doubtful that Spot could take his place.

"Keep your tail still when you bark," he told the old dog. "These farmyard fowls won't pay much attention to you if they see your tail a-wagging."

"I'll remember what you say," Spot answered.

"Be sure to keep a sharp eye on that Rooster." Turkey Proudfoot went on. "I don't want him to get the idea into his head that he's running things in this, farmyard."

"Very well!" said Spot. "Shall I let him crow a bit, if he wants to?"

"Let him crow—yes!" Turkey Proudfoot answered. "But if he starts to gobbling—well, you'd better send for me at once."

"What about the Peacock?" Spot inquired wickedly. He knew that Turkey Proudfoot was frightfully jealous of Johnnie Green's newest pet.

"The Peacock!" Turkey Proudfoot squawked. "Pull out his tail feathers— every one of them! I've been intending to do that myself. But I've been so busy that I haven't had the time for it."

Then they said good-by.

"You ought to tell me where you're going," Spot suggested. "If the Rooster should gobble I must know where to find you."

So Turkey Proudfoot told him. He told him in such a low tone that nobody else could hear.

XXIV

BROTHER TOM

IT was almost dark in the cornfield on a crisp evening late in November. It was not Farmer Green's field, but that of a neighbor of his. And it was far from any house.

The pumpkins had been gathered weeks before. The cornstalks had long since been cut and now stood in shocks amidst the stubble.

On the whole, the scene was bleak and dismal. Not a creature moved anywhere. Even the meadow, mice had already found the nights too chilly for their liking. Turkey Proudfoot was there alone, standing like a statue, as if he were waiting for somebody.

"I don't see where he can be," Turkey Proudfoot muttered. "I've spent three days and three nights here already. And he has never been late before in all the years that I've been coming here for my vacation."

At last Turkey Proudfoot bestirred himself. With a hop, skip and a jump he landed on top of the rail fence that surrounded the field and settled himself for the night.

He had scarcely closed his eyes when a faint "Gobble, gobble, gobble" from across the cornfield drove all idea of sleep out of his head. He started up, stretched his long neck as high as he could, and burst forth with a deafening "Gobble, gobble, gobble!" Then he paused and listened.

The answer soon reached him. It was nearer this time. And after Turkey Proudfoot had repeated his interesting remark about a dozen times a huge old turkey cock came running up and alighted, panting, upon the fence-rail where Turkey Proudfoot was roosting.

"You're late," Turkey Proudfoot greeted him. "I'd begun to fear that you had met with an accident. What kept you?"

"They shut me up in a pen," the newcomer told him. He was still somewhat out of breath, partly because of rage at having been imprisoned, partly

51

because he had been hurrying. "They shut me up two days ago," he explained.

"Ah!" Turkey Proudfoot exclaimed. "You ought to have left home three days ago. Did you forget our yearly meeting?"

"No!" said the other. "But I must have miscounted the days."

"That's very dangerous at this time of year," Turkey Proudfoot replied. "It's a wonder that you escaped from the pen. How did you manage to slip out!"

"Somebody left the door ajar," said the strange turkey.

"Ah! I've always claimed that our family was lucky!" Turkey Proudfoot cried. And he gave his companion a slap on the back with his wing.

Now, that was a jolly thing to do — and not at all like Turkey Proudfoot. But he was glad to see the newcomer. They were brothers. They had been separated when quite young; and they had lived on neighboring farms all their lives.

For a time they talked together pleasantly enough. Of course Turkey Proudfoot couldn't help boasting about the way he ruled the roost when he was at home. But his brother Tom was just as great a boaster. And after a time each began to think the other's stories somewhat tiresome. So they began to yawn. And at last they fell asleep.

A crescent moon peeped down at them from a clear, cold sky that crackled with stars. A chilling breeze swept down the valley. And sometime during the night Turkey Proudfoot woke up and found himself a-shiver. He sidled along the rail and huddled against his brother Tom.

Brother Tom stirred and stretched himself.

"This night's a nipper, isn't it?" he remarked. "I can't help wishing my legs were like Mr. Grouse's."

"Huh!" Turkey Proudfoot exclaimed. "You'd look queer — as fat as you are — if you had legs as short as his."

"Ah! But his legs are feathered out. And there's nothing like feathers to keep the cold off," said Brother Tom.

"I suppose," said Turkey Proudfoot, "Mr. Grouse's legs wouldn't get as cold as ours do, even if he hadn't a feather on them."

"Why not?" asked Brother Tom.

"Because they're shorter," said Turkey Proudfoot.

Brother Tom made no reply. He was no longer awake.

Being on the leeward side of his brother, Turkey Proudfoot began to feel warmer.

"I'm glad Tom's a big fellow," he murmured drowsily. "He makes a fine windbreak." Then he too fell asleep.

And the next day was Thanksgiving.

THE END